R0110175155

04/2018

D1399620

No Biz Like Show Biz

For Danny, whose talent is unlimited!—N.K.

For Geoffrey.—J&W

GROSSET & DUNLAP
Published by the Penguin Group
Penguin Group (USA) Inc., 375 Hudson Street,
New York, New York 10014, U.S.A.
Penguin Group (Canada), 90 Eglinton Avenue East, Suite 700,
Toronto, Ontario, Canada M4P 2Y3
(a division of Pearson Penguin Canada Inc.)
Penguin Books Ltd, 80 Strand, London WC2R 0RL, England
Penguin Ireland, 25 St Stephen's Green, Dublin 2, Ireland
(a division of Penguin Books Ltd)
Penguin Group (Australia), 250 Camberwell Road,
Camberwell, Victoria 3124, Australia
(a division of Pearson Australia Group Pty Ltd)
Penguin Books India Pvt Ltd, 11 Community Centre,
Panchsheel Park, New Delhi - 110 017, India
Penguin Group (NZ), Cnr Airborne and Rosedale Roads,
Albany, Auckland 1310, New Zealand
(a division of Pearson New Zealand Ltd)
Penguin Books (South Africa) (Pty) Ltd, 24 Sturdee Avenue,
Rosebank, Johannesburg 2196, South Africa

Penguin Books Ltd, Registered Offices:
80 Strand, London WC2R 0RL, England

Library of Congress Control Number: 2006029448

ISBN 978-0-448-44440-6   10 9 8 7

KATIE KAZOO, SWITCHEROO

No Biz Like Show Biz

by Nancy Krulik • illustrated by John & Wendy

Grosset & Dunlap

Chapter 1

"Ma may mi mo moo!" Suzanne sang out as she stood in the middle of Katie Carew's kitchen.

It was Thursday afternoon. Suzanne and some of the other fourth-grade kids had come over after school. They were going to bake cookies with Katie's mom. Everyone knew Mrs. Carew baked the most delicious cookies in Cherrydale.

"Ma may mi mo moo!" Suzanne sang again, louder this time.

"What weird language is that?" Jeremy asked Suzanne.

"Jeremy, you don't know anything,"

Suzanne said, tossing her long brown hair behind her shoulder.

"I know one thing. You sound terrible!" Jeremy clapped his hands over his ears.

"Come on you guys, stop it," Katie said with a sigh. She really hated it when her two best friends fought. "We're here to bake sugar cookies with my mom."

"Exactly," Miriam Chan agreed.

"We should get started. We have to bake enough for all the kids at the shelter," Emma Weber added.

"I know," Katie said. "My mom wants to drive the cookies over tonight."

"Don't worry, Katie Kazoo," George Brennan assured Katie, using the way-cool nickname he had given her in third grade. He held up an apron. "We're ready for action. At least, *most* of us are. Suzanne is apparently here to moo like a cow."

"I am not mooing like a cow," Suzanne insisted. "I'm doing my singing exercises."

"You mean your croaking exercises," Kevin Camilleri added.

"Come on," Katie said. "That's not nice."

"I don't care what you boys think," Suzanne told George, Kevin, and Jeremy. "I'll have the last laugh when I get the lead in the fourth-grade musical."

The tryouts for *A Wacky Winter Wonder-*

land were tomorrow. Katie knew Suzanne had her heart set on the part of the Snow Fairy.

"The Snow Fairy has to sing some big solos in the show," Suzanne went on.

"Oh, I definitely think you should sing solo," George told Suzanne.

"You do?" Suzanne sounded surprised.

"Sure," George said. "*So low* we can't hear you!"

Kevin and Jeremy started to laugh.

Suzanne turned to Katie. "I'm a really good singer . . . Aren't I?" she asked.

"You, um . . . you have a *special* singing voice. No one sounds quite like you," Katie replied. She quickly headed toward the refrigerator for the cookie dough.

Suzanne scowled at Jeremy, George, and Kevin.

"I'm going to get that part. You'll see!" she told them.

"Yeah, you wish!" Kevin replied.

Katie stopped in her tracks. "She does *not*

wish!" she exclaimed.

Everyone stopped and stared at her.

"What are you so upset about?" George asked.

Katie blushed. She didn't know what to say. Katie hated wishes. And she had good reason to.

Unfortunately, she couldn't tell her friends what that reason was. They wouldn't believe her, anyway.

Chapter 2

It had all started one really bad day last year when Katie was in third grade. At recess Katie had dropped the football in the middle of a big play and lost the game for her team. Then she'd stepped in a puddle and splattered mud all over her favorite pants. Things got even worse when she burped really loudly in front of the whole class.

That night Katie wished she could be anyone other than herself.

There must have been a shooting star overhead when she made that wish, because the very next day her wish came true. The magic wind arrived and turned Katie into Speedy, the hamster in her third-grade class! Katie spent the whole morning going round and round on a hamster wheel and gnawing on chew sticks!

The magic wind came back again and again after that. Sometimes it changed Katie into other kids, like Jeremy, Suzanne, and even Suzanne's baby sister, Heather.

The magic wind didn't just turn Katie into kids and animals. It turned her into grown-ups, too. Like the time Katie had been switcherooed into her favorite author, Nellie Farrow. It happened right before Nellie was supposed to talk to the fourth grade about her new book. The trouble was, Katie hadn't read the book yet. Because of Katie, Nellie had looked like a fool in front of everybody!

As far as Katie was concerned, wishes brought nothing but trouble.

"Let's stop talking about singing, okay?" she finally told her friends. "And let's get started baking."

Mrs. Carew came in just then and started handing out baking trays and utensils.

"Mrs. Carew, will you let *us* eat some of the cookies, too?" George asked Katie's mom.

Katie laughed. George had never met a sweet he didn't want to eat.

"Sure," Katie's mother told him. "How else will we know if they're good?"

"Cool," George said, tying on his apron. "Let's get started."

Chapter 3

"Sorry I can't stay to help clean up," Suzanne said as she put on her coat and began walking out of the kitchen. The cookies were cooling on the counter.

"Hey, that's not fair," Kevin said.

"I have to work on my song for tomorrow's auditions," Suzanne explained. "And then I have to practice my turns for modeling class. I'm supposed to do that ten minutes every day."

George rolled his eyes. "Oh, give me a break. How hard can it be to turn?" He stood up on his toes and spun around quickly.

Crash! Clang! George bumped into the kitchen counter. A pile of baking tins fell to the floor.

"*That* hard," Suzanne told him smugly. "See you all tomorrow."

"She always has to leave right when it's time to clean up," Jeremy complained.

Miriam Chan turned on the water in the sink and began to wash out a mixing bowl. Then suddenly she began singing a Bayside

Boys song as she scraped the batter away. "I dream of you when I'm awake. I hope that doesn't sound too fake . . ."

"Wow, you have a great voice!" Katie exclaimed. She smiled broadly. The Bayside Boys were her favorite band, and "Dreams" was one of their best songs.

Miriam blushed. "I didn't even realize I was singing out loud," she said, looking very embarrassed. "I like to sing when I do chores. It's something my mom taught me to do. It makes the work go faster."

"Miriam, you should *totally* try out for the solo in the holiday show," Katie suggested.

"Yeah. You'd be so much better than Suzanne," George told her. He lifted his head up and pretended to sing like Suzanne. "Moo! Moo!"

"Arooo!" Katie's chocolate-brown-and-white cocker spaniel, Pepper, howled and buried his ears in his paws.

"Oh, I could never sing in front of people," Miriam said. She pulled nervously at her straight black hair.

"Sure you could," Emma W. told her. "You

just sang in front of us."

"That's different," Miriam explained, blushing. "I could never get up on a stage and sing."

"Why not?" George asked her. "It's just singing in a different place."

"All those people staring at me . . ." Miriam made a face.

"My big brother, Ian, had a part in the middle school play last month," Kevin said. "He was *really* nervous. But my dad told him to imagine all the people in the audience in their underwear. Then he wasn't scared anymore."

George started laughing. "Imagine Mrs. *Jerk*man in her underwear. Oooo."

Katie, Jeremy, and Kevin all started to giggle, imagining Mrs. Derkman, who had been their strict third-grade teacher—and also happened to be Katie's next-door neighbor—in her underwear.

Miriam laughed a little, too.

"See," Kevin told her. "It works."

"I guess," Miriam said slowly. "But I can't just get up and audition. I haven't rehearsed anything. And the tryouts are tomorrow!"

"You could practice at my house right now," Kevin suggested. "We have the music for lots of songs in our piano bench. My mom could play the piano while you sing."

"I don't know," Miriam said nervously.

"We'll go to Kevin's with you," Katie assured her. "We'll be your practice audience."

"Just don't imagine me in my underwear," George warned.

"I promise, George. I won't," Miriam vowed, giggling.

Chapter 4

"I hope Miriam tries out," Jeremy said as he and Katie walked to school together the next morning.

"Me too," Katie agreed.

"I can't believe we never heard her sing before. I mean, we've known her our whole lives . . ." Jeremy began. He stopped suddenly when they reached the playground. "Oh, man. Check out Suzanne."

Katie turned and spotted Suzanne strolling toward them. She was wearing the weirdest outfit—shimmery purple and silver pants; a shiny silver jacket; long, glittery earrings; and lots and lots of silver beads.

"What's that about?" Katie wondered out loud.

Jeremy shrugged. "You're asking *me*? She's your friend, not mine."

"Wow!" Jessica Haynes exclaimed as she ran over to Suzanne. "You look like a rock star."

Suzanne beamed. "Well, I *am* about to become a star," she told Jessica. "At the tryouts, Mr. Guthrie will know I'm a real singer the minute he sees me."

By now a whole crowd of kids, including Miriam, had gathered around Suzanne.

"And he'll realize you're *not* a real singer the minute you open your mouth," George told Suzanne. "Besides, Miriam's going to be the Snow Fairy."

"Miriam?" Suzanne asked, surprised. She

turned around and stared at her. "I didn't know *you* were trying out."

"Well, I-I might," Miriam stammered nervously. "I haven't actually decided if—"

"She's got a beautiful voice," Emma W. told Suzanne.

Suzanne grabbed Katie by the arm and started to pull her toward the school building. "Miriam will never get the solo," Suzanne whispered. "Look at her. She's wearing blue jeans and sneakers. She doesn't look anything like a singer."

"Suzanne, it's not about the clothes," Katie tried to explain.

But Suzanne didn't care what Katie had to say. Instead, she went running over to Jessica. "Oooh, Jess, I want you to put my hair in a French braid," she said.

As Suzanne and Jessica walked away, George shook his head. "French braid?" he said. "She could wear French *bread* on her head and she still wouldn't get that part."

That afternoon while the other kids were on the playground for recess, Katie had to stay inside and do math. That was because instead of finishing her math work that morning, Katie had drawn pictures all over the paper.

"I'm sorry, Mr. G.," Katie apologized as she stared at the half-finished work sheet.

Mr. G. looked down at Katie's white sneakers. She had used a blue pen to draw lots of hearts and flowers all over them. "Did you doodle on those, too?" he asked.

Katie nodded. "My mom was kind of mad."

"I'll bet she was," Mr. G. replied. He smiled at Katie. "You're a very good artist."

"Thanks," Katie said. She liked it when her teacher complimented her.

"But you have to learn when and where to draw," Mr. G. continued. "Math class is not the right time. And your work sheet is not the right place. Neither are your sneakers."

"I know," Katie said quietly.

"I think I know a place where you can put your talent to good use," he assured her. "Katie, would you like to design the scenery for the play?"

Would she ever!

× × ×

When it was time to go home, Katie passed by the auditorium. There was a line of kids standing in the hall. They were waiting their turns to audition for parts in *Wacky Winter Wonderland*.

Suzanne was at the front of the line, of course. Her hair was in a French braid, and she was practicing her singing. "Ma mi moooooooooo," she howled.

George was in line also. So was Kadeem. Mandy Banks was trying out for the chorus along with Zoe Canter. Jeremy and Kevin were sitting at the end of the line, playing cards while they waited their turns.

"Are you trying out for the show?" Jeremy asked Katie.

Katie shook her head. "I'm working on the scenery. I'm going to design some of the backdrops and paint."

"Cool," Jeremy told her. "You're good at art."

"It was Mr. G.'s idea," Katie admitted. "He thought it would be better if I drew scenery instead of doodling all over my math."

"Why is this taking so long?" Kevin groaned. "I hate waiting."

Katie looked at the long line of kids. There was someone missing. "Where's Miriam?" she asked nervously. "Didn't she show up?"

"Not yet," Jeremy said.

"I hope she hasn't chickened out," Katie replied. "She's got such a great voice."

"I didn't chicken out," Miriam said, walking up behind Katie.

"Oops, sorry, Miriam," Katie said apologetically. "I wasn't calling you a chicken. I just was worried you got scared."

"I almost *did* chicken out," Miriam admitted. "But I figured I kind of owed you guys. I mean, you spent so much time listening to me sing and everything."

Just then the auditorium door swung open. Mr. G. poked his head out. "Okay, dudes," he said. "Let's get this started. Suzanne, you're up first."

"Okay," Suzanne told him. "Just let me warm up my voice." She cleared her throat. "Ma mo me mo. Ta to te to."

Jeremy made a pained face. George stuck his fingers in his ears.

But Katie would never do anything mean like that. "Good luck, Suzanne," she called to her.

"Oh, I don't need luck," Suzanne assured her. "I've got talent. I'm going in there a fourth-grader and coming out a Snow Fairy!"

Chapter 5

"I got it! I got it!"

Katie held the phone away from her ear. The person on the other end was screaming frantically.

"Got *what*?" Katie asked.

"I got the part!"

"Congratulations," Katie said into the telephone receiver. "Who is this?"

"Oops. Sorry." The voice grew quiet. "It's me, Miriam. I got the part. I'm the Snow Fairy in *Wacky Winter Wonderland*."

Now it was Katie's turn to scream. "Wow! That's so amazing!"

"Th—thanks," Miriam told her. "I have

lots of lines to learn—and three solos."

Katie couldn't tell if Miriam was scared or happy.

"You're going to be really great," Katie assured her.

"I have to practice a lot," Miriam said. "I want to be perfect."

"I'll get to hear you," Katie told her. "I'm on the stage crew."

"Oh, cool," Miriam said. She grew quiet for a moment. Then she added, "I can't believe it, Katie. Of all the people who tried out, Mr. Guthrie picked me."

Miriam definitely sounded more scared than happy.

Katie frowned. She bet there was one person who wasn't so happy right now— Suzanne.

A few minutes after she hung up with Miriam, Katie's telephone began to ring again. "Hello?" she said as she picked up the receiver.

"I can't believe it!" the person on the other end shouted into Katie's ear.

"Hello, Suzanne," Katie said.

"Mr. G. picked Miriam Chan to be the Snow Fairy," Suzanne continued without even saying hi back.

"I'm sorry you didn't get the part you wanted," Katie said.

"I'm stuck being a snowflake," Suzanne told her. "Me? A snowflake! I have to lead a bunch of kindergartners onstage. They'll be the little snowflakes. Can you believe it? I'll be dressed like a kindergartner while Miriam is up there playing *my* part."

"Suzanne, that wasn't your part. It was up to Mr. G. to decide," Katie reminded her.

"Whatever," Suzanne replied with a sigh. "Maybe Miriam will get sick. Then I can be the Snow Fairy."

"What do you mean?" Katie asked her.

"I'm her understudy. I have to learn all her lines and all her songs, just in case." Suzanne groaned. "I don't know who told Miriam to try out. But when I find out . . ."

Katie gulped. She crossed her fingers that Suzanne would never find out.

Because when Suzanne was angry, she could start a real blizzard of trouble.

Chapter 6

"We need to attach the sun to a wire so it can move across the sky," Mr. G. called back-stage to Katie. "Can you do that?"

"I'm working on it now. Don't worry. I'll have it ready before the dress rehearsal," Katie shouted back. That was still two weeks away. She smiled proudly. Since rehearsals had begun, she'd learned a lot about how to make scenery look real.

"Great," Mr. G. told her. He leaned back in his chair and turned to the stage. "Now let's take this scene from the top. It's time for the Snowman Shuffle. This is an important scene because it's when the Wicked Wind Monster comes and freezes everything—maybe forever!"

George laughed. "This play is really wild, Mr. G.," he told him. "Where did you come up with a story about a Wicked Wind Monster who threatens to freeze the planet?"

"I don't know, dude," Mr. G. chuckled. "It's the magic of imagination. And that's my favorite nation."

George grinned. Mr. G. said that all the time.

"Okay, Kadeem, you're the Wicked Wind Monster. It's time for you to blow onto the stage."

Katie stood next to Miriam and watched from the wings.

Kadeem Carter began to wave his hands wildly as he moved. "Whoosh," he said. Then he puckered his lips and blew. "Here I come, freezing everything in sight. That's good news for you, *Snowman*."

"All that cold air is sure making me

hungry," George said. He was the Snowman. "I could go for an *iceberg*-er!"

Katie couldn't help laughing. Some of the kids in the chorus began to laugh, too.

"Hey, that's not your line," Kadeem told him. "I know every line in this play. You're supposed to say, 'Brrr . . . thanks for the help.'"

"I know," George admitted. "But my joke's funnier."

Mr. G. shook his head. "Stick to the script, George."

George frowned.

"Let's start over," the teacher said.

Kadeem went back to his spot and began waving his arms again. "Here I come, freezing everything in sight. That's good news for you, *Snowman*," he repeated.

"Brrr—" George began to say his line.

But Kadeem interrupted him. He opened his mouth really wide and pretended to nip at George's arm.

"Hey, what's that about?" George demanded.

"Frost*bite*," Kadeem said. He began to laugh.

George frowned. "That's not his line," he called out to Mr. G.

"No, it's not," Mr. G. agreed. "Can't you two just say the lines the way you're supposed to?"

George and Kadeem stared at each other.

Mr. G. sighed. "Okay, let's move on. Suzanne, bring the kindergarten snowflakes onstage."

Katie watched Suzanne take one of the kindergarten snowflakes by the hand and practically drag her across the stage. The other little flakes followed.

"Mr. Guthrie, this isn't working for me," Suzanne said, stopping suddenly.

"What do you mean?" Mr. G. asked her, surprised.

"I just don't feel the part. I can't get into

the Snowflake's head," Suzanne explained.

Katie and Miriam looked at each other and rolled their eyes.

"That's because snowflakes don't have heads," George reminded her. "I think your brain's melting, Suzanne."

"You don't know anything about acting," Suzanne told George. "I have to be able to understand my character in order to play her."

"Okay," Mr. G. said. "So how about this? You're a snowflake who is really, really excited to finally come down to earth."

"How excited?" Suzanne asked him.

"Um . . . as excited as you would be if your picture were on a magazine cover," he suggested.

But Suzanne wasn't listening anymore. She was staring at Katie and Miriam in the wings. As she took the kindergartners backstage so they could start again, she ran right up to Miriam.

"Are you okay?" Suzanne asked her. "You

don't look so good."

"I don't?" Miriam asked. "I feel all right."

Katie looked curiously at Suzanne. "Miriam looks fine to me," she said.

Suzanne avoided Katie's stare. "Well, Miriam looks green to me. Like she's going to throw up or something." She paused and turned to Miriam. "Please tell us you didn't eat the squiggly pasta at lunch today!"

"Yeah, I did," Miriam said. She sounded worried. "Why?"

"Oh, it's nothing. I heard a worm got stuck in the pot," Suzanne continued. "It was probably just a rumor, though. Of course, eating a wiggly, squiggly worm *could* make someone kind of sick—"

"Suzanne! Stop talking about yucky stuff!" Katie said. She knew creepy, crawly things like worms really grossed Miriam out. Everyone in the fourth grade knew that.

And now Miriam's face really did turn kind of green. She clapped her hand over her mouth. "I'll be back," Miriam groaned. "I don't feel so good."

Suzanne smiled triumphantly as Miriam ran to the restroom backstage. "Gee, I hope she's okay," she said. "But if she's not, I know all her lines. I'm ready to take over."

Chapter 7

"Okay, now carefully pull the sun across the stage," Mr. G. told Katie. Katie nodded and, with her teacher's help, began to pull the thick ropes that were attached to the heavy wooden sun. It had taken more than a week for Katie to draw, paint, and attach the piece of scenery to the ropes. But now it was ready to go.

And just in time. After long weeks of rehearsals, the show was just two days away!

"Wow, it's working!" Katie squealed with delight as she stood offstage.

"That was perfect!" Mr. G. told her. "It looks like the sun is actually moving across the sky."

"We did it!" Katie told her teacher.

Mr. G. shook his head. "No, *you* did it, Katie."

She smiled proudly.

Mr. G. looked down at Katie's new red sneakers. There wasn't one drawing on them anywhere. "You're not doodling as much, are you?"

Katie shook her head. "Just when I'm watching TV or talking on the phone or something."

"Your scenery is really wonderful, Katie," Mr. G. told her. "The crystal icicles you hung on the curtains and the wooden trees are amazing. They shimmer like the real thing. What a great idea! And the drawing you did of the frozen lake for the backdrop is really spectacular."

She smiled proudly. "Thanks," she replied. "I . . ."

But Katie's voice was drowned out by the

sound of the piano. Miriam was about to sing.

"Snowballs rock! We're on a roll. He can freeze the planet, but not our souls," Miriam sang. "So don't be frightened. Don't take the Wicked Wind Monster's jive. The Snow Fairy's here, and we will survive!"

Katie grinned. Miriam was really good. She was going to be a big hit in the show. Everyone knew it.

But Miriam didn't brag about getting the lead part or having a great voice, like Suzanne would have if *she'd* gotten the Snow Fairy role. Miriam was too shy and quiet to do that.

Well, *usually* she was shy and quiet. Somehow, once she got onstage, Miriam changed. You could hear her singing all the way from the back of the auditorium.

"Winter's wild, a wacky time," Miriam sang out, dancing around the stage and waving her arms. "But sooner or later, the sun's gotta shine. Mark my words. It's gonna shine."

Katie couldn't believe it. Just a few weeks ago, Katie, Emma, George, Kevin, and Jeremy practically had to beg Miriam to practice one little song. And now she was singing and dancing all around the stage.

As Miriam finished her song, everyone began to clap. "That was great," Mr. G. told Miriam.

"Thank you," she said. "I've been practicing really hard."

"I can tell." Then Mr. G. told her to go backstage to the girls' dressing room. "Ms. Sweet has finished your costume. She'd like you to try it on."

"Okay," Miriam replied quietly. She was back to her usual shy self.

As Miriam walked by, Katie smiled at her. "Your voice sounds amazing," she told her.

"Thanks." Miriam smiled. "Your sun *looks* amazing."

"Thanks," Katie replied. "You know, before

that day at my house, I didn't know you could sing. I guess we still have a lot of stuff to learn about each other."

Just then Suzanne came walking over to the girls. "I saw the greatest movie on TV last night," she remarked casually.

"Really?" Miriam replied. "What was it called?"

"The Phantom of the Opera," Suzanne told her. "It was a really old movie."

"What was it about?" Miriam asked Suzanne.

"This creepy guy with only half a face who lives underneath a theater in Paris," Suzanne told her. "He's really crazy. He wants to kill people, and he kidnaps the girl who is the star of the opera."

Miriam gulped. "He lives under a *theater*?"

Suzanne nodded and looked around. "Come to think of it, the stage in the movie looked a little bit like this one."

"Suzanne, stop it," Katie warned.

"Yeah, I don't think I want to hear any more," Miriam added.

"But it was so scary," Suzanne continued. "And you know what, the girl in the movie— the one who had the lead part—had straight black hair just like yours, Miriam."

Miriam gulped.

"Come on, Suzanne. There's no phantom

hiding here," Katie insisted.

"That's exactly what they kept saying in the movie! 'There's no phantom hiding here,'" Suzanne exclaimed.

Miriam gulped and bit her lip nervously. A few beads of sweat began to form on her forehead.

Just then Mr. G. walked backstage. "There you are, Miriam," he said. "Ms. Sweet is waiting with your costume."

"Y-yes, sir." Miriam looked like she was about to cry.

As Miriam headed out of the auditorium, Katie turned to Suzanne. "Why did you start talking about that movie? You know how scared Miriam gets."

"Miriam is scared of everything." Suzanne pressed her lips together. "Who knows? She might even get too scared to go on the night of the show."

Katie's eyes grew wide. Now she was certain about what Suzanne was up to. She was trying to scare Miriam out of the play so she could take over the lead part. "Suzanne, leave Miriam alone!" Katie shouted.

Suzanne shook her head. "I don't know what you're talking about," she insisted. "I wasn't doing anything to Miriam. I was just talking about a movie I saw. Miriam shouldn't worry about a phantom *or* stage fright. If she's not here, she's got a talented understudy to go on for her. She's very lucky."

Katie rolled her eyes. *Lucky* wasn't exactly the word she would have chosen.

Chapter 8

The next afternoon, Katie hurried to the auditorium right after school was over. She wanted to get there as quickly as possible to get ready for the dress rehearsal.

The dress rehearsal was very important. Today all the actors would perform the play in their costumes. They would run through the whole show without stopping, whether or not they made any mistakes.

Now that the play was just one day away, Katie was getting kind of nervous. She wasn't really sure how it was all going to work out. But Katie could tell Miriam wasn't nervous at all. She had no reason to be. She knew her part really well. She had been rehearsing every day, singing her songs and going over her lines with her best friend, Zoe Canter. Even now, she was practicing one of her songs on the stage.

"Get out of my way, you Wicked Wind Monster. Blow right out of town. It's time for spring to rock your world. The sun's gonna knock the wind down!" she sang.

Katie smiled. Miriam was going to be amazing!

"Okay, dudes," Katie heard Mr. G. say as he walked into the auditorium. "Let's get this show on the road. Everyone go to the dressing rooms and put on your costumes."

All the cast members headed backstage, leaving Katie alone in the auditorium. She poured some glue over the branches of one of the wooden pine trees she and Mr. G. had built. Then she sprinkled green and silver glitter onto the glue.

There. That would make the trees look all

sparkly and wintry.

Just then Katie felt a cool breeze blowing on her neck. *Gosh, it's chilly in here,* Katie thought. She turned to see if someone had left a window open.

But all the windows were shut tight.

The curtains weren't rustling in the breeze.

In fact, the wind seemed to be blowing only around Katie. Which could mean only one thing.

This was no ordinary wind. This was the magic wind! Katie was about to turn into someone else!

"Oh no!" she shouted into the tornado that was suddenly whirling around her. "Not now. Not right before the dress rehearsal!"

But the magic wind didn't care about the school play. It came whenever it wanted to. And it changed Katie into whomever it wanted to. Switcheroo!

Suddenly the wild tornado stopped. The magic wind was gone.

And so was Katie Carew.

She'd been turned into somebody else.

But who?

Chapter 9

"Miriam, there you are," Ms. Sweet, the other fourth-grade teacher, said as she walked into the auditorium. "I want to make sure your wings will stay on the back of your costume."

Katie turned around quickly, looking for Miriam. But there didn't seem to be anyone else but Ms. Sweet.

And herself, of course.

"Miriam, are you okay?" Ms. Sweet asked.

Katie gasped. Ms. Sweet seemed to be looking right at her. Katie glanced down. Instead of her red sneakers, Katie was wearing a pair of soft, pink dancing shoes. And she had on a sparkly white dress.

Miriam Chan's costume!

Oh no! Katie had turned into Miriam Chan!

"But I can't . . ." she began. "I mean, I'm not . . ." Katie stopped. She wasn't sure what to say. She couldn't tell Ms. Sweet that she wasn't really Miriam Chan. The teacher would never believe her.

Katie wouldn't have believed it either if it hadn't happened to her.

"Come on, Miriam," Ms. Sweet urged her gently.

"Um . . . okay," Katie said quietly.

Just then Suzanne came bursting back onstage. "Ms. Sweet!" she shouted excitedly. "I can't find my snowflake crown."

"I'll be with you in a minute, Suzanne," Ms. Sweet replied patiently. "I just have to help Miriam with her wings."

"But Ms. Sweet, you have to help *me* first," Suzanne insisted. "Think about it. No one has ever really seen a fairy. Miriam can wear one wing or no wings, and no one will know if something's wrong. But everyone has seen a snowflake before. My costume has to be perfect!"

Ms. Sweet sighed. "Suzanne, stop being such a drama queen. I'll be with you as soon as I help Miriam with these wings."

The moment her teacher turned around, Suzanne made a face and glared angrily at Miriam. But Katie couldn't think about Suzanne right now. She had to try and concentrate on being Miriam.

The problem was, Katie hadn't paid close attention to the rehearsals. Most of the time she had been backstage working with Mr. G. That had taken all of her concentration.

But Katie had to do something. She couldn't just run away. If she left now, Miriam might lose her part. That wouldn't be fair. Not after she had worked so hard.

Katie was going to have to try and get through the rehearsal as best she could. And if she had to make up a few words, it would be okay. After all, George and Kadeem did it all the time.

"Hi, Miriam," Mr. G. greeted Katie. "Have you seen Katie?"

Katie gulped. How was she supposed to answer that?

"She's supposed to help me with the scenery," Mr. G. continued.

"Katie, well, uh . . ." Katie began nervously. "I, um . . . I saw her. But . . . um . . . she's not here now . . . exactly."

"Exactly?" Mr. G. asked, confused.

"Well, I mean, she put the glitter on the trees like you told her to, but she said she still had some props to find. So she left to . . . um . . . look for them," Katie said quickly.

"Oh," Mr. G. said. "No problem. I can handle things till she gets back. If you see her, just tell her to go straight up to the catwalk."

"Sure," Katie told him. "No problem."

As Mr. G. walked away, Katie frowned.

She hated lying to her teacher. But what else could she have done?

And maybe, if she was really lucky, the magic wind would come back soon to turn her into Katie again.

Chapter 10

No such luck!

That was all Katie could think as the curtain went up on the dress rehearsal.

There was no way the magic wind was going to come back now that everyone was onstage. The magic wind only came when Katie was all alone.

"One, two, a one, two, three, four!" Mr. Starkey shouted as he started to play his piano.

"Miriam, go," Ms. Sweet said, gently pushing Katie out onto the stage. "It's your entrance."

Katie gulped as she did her best to dance

onto the stage, whirling and twirling the way she thought Miriam was supposed to do it.

"Winter rocks," Katie sang out. She paused for a minute, trying to remember the next words of Miriam's song.

"Don't stop," Mr. G. called to her. "Just keep going. If you can't remember, make something up."

"Winter rocks, like, um . . . a fox in socks. Or snowballs in a box," Katie sang in a shaky voice.

"*Snowballs in a box?* What's up with her?" she heard Kadeem say to George.

"She's not hitting any of the right notes, either," Kevin added, loud enough for Katie to hear. Thank goodness the Winter Chorus began to sing with her. At least now no one could hear what a mess she was making of the words.

But everyone could see that Katie didn't know any of the dance moves. She kept banging into the scenery and the other actors.

"Ow!" George shouted out. "Miriam, you just kicked me in the leg."

"Sorry," Katie told him.

"George, you have to stay in character," Suzanne shouted at him, trying to sound like a real actress. "Snowmen don't have legs."

"Well, this one does," George told her angrily. "And Miriam just kicked my right one."

Mr. Guthrie sighed heavily. "Let's move on, everyone. Miriam, keep singing."

But Katie didn't want to sing. She wanted to cry. Or run away. Or something. Anything but sing and dance on that stage. She just stood there, frozen.

"Remember," Jeremy whispered to her. "Picture everybody in their underwear."

Katie tried; she really did. But even picturing her teacher in his boxers didn't make her any less scared.

Just then, Kadeem, all dressed up in his dark gray Wicked Wind Monster costume,

whooshed onto the stage. He waved his arms around wildly. "Here I come, freezing everything in sight," he howled. "That's good news for you, *Snowman*."

"Brrr . . . Thanks for the help," George answered.

"Snowman, you're one cold dude!" the chorus began singing to a rock beat. "But that Wicked Wind is really rude. The lakes are frozen and the mountains, too. So what are we supposed to do? Our tears will freeze if we start to cry. Oh, look, here come some of your pals falling down from the sky . . ."

Just then Suzanne raced onto the stage in her snowy white tutu. Behind her she dragged a long line of kindergartners.

Katie moved out of the way as Suzanne and the younger kids began to twirl around.

"We're snowflakes, and we—" Suzanne began.

"*Oomf,*" Katie exclaimed as she banged the back of her head into one of the wooden pine trees that she had placed in the corner of the stage.

Crash! The wooden tree fell to the floor so hard, the stage shook.

"Miriam! Stop ruining my scene," Suzanne shouted at her.

"Who's out of character now, Suzanne?" George said.

Suzanne stuck her tongue out at George.

One of the kindergartners began to cry.

"What's wrong, James?" Mr. G. asked.

"I have to pee . . . real bad!" James shouted. He raced off the stage.

"I don't think he's going to make it in time," Kadeem said.

"There's gonna be some yellow snow." George giggled.

Mr. G. put his head in his hands. "That's it. Let's take a five-minute break, and then we'll start this dress rehearsal all over again."

"I sure hope Miriam does better when we

start over," Katie overheard George say to Kevin.

"I know," Kevin agreed. "She was awful."

Katie frowned. Kevin was right, and she knew it. She also knew that she wasn't going to sound any better in five minutes.

Katie definitely did not want to go back up on that stage. She felt really bad for Miriam, but she just couldn't do it.

It looked like Suzanne's dream was finally going to come true.

Chapter 11

"Okay, everybody, take your places on the stage," Mr. G. shouted out five minutes later.

Instantly, the kids ran to the stage. Katie opened her mouth wide to sing and . . .

Nothing came out. Not a sound. "Miriam!" Mr. G. shouted as he climbed down from the catwalk. "What's wrong?"

Katie pointed to her throat. "I think I've lost my voice," she said in a hoarse whisper.

"Are you sure?" Mr. G. asked her.

Katie nodded. "Can't talk," she whispered.

"Somebody get her some tea with lemon and honey!" Mr. Starkey suggested.

"I'll get it." Ms. Sweet hurried over to Katie. "You come with me, Miriam."

As Katie walked off the stage, she heard Mr. G. say, "Okay, Suzanne, you'll have to take Miriam's place for the dress rehearsal."

"No problem!" Suzanne's grin went from ear to ear.

Katie was silent as she followed Ms. Sweet to the cafeteria. Of course, she hadn't really lost her voice. She'd just pretended so she could get off the stage. "Thanks," she said in a hoarse whisper as she took a cup of tea from the teacher.

"Shh . . . don't try to talk," Ms. Sweet warned. "Let's go back to the auditorium now. You can watch from the audience while you sip that tea."

✕　✕　✕

As she sat down in the auditorium, Katie could hear Suzanne singing away. She was kind of off-key and out of tune, but at least she was getting the words right.

"Snowballs rock! We're on a roll. He can freeze the planet, but not our souls," she sang.

"So don't be frightened. Don't take the Wicked Wind Monster's jive. The Snow Fairy's here, and we will survive!" Suzanne sang out as she danced around the stage, waving Miriam's fairy wand and smiling happily.

Suzanne was sure having a good time. And the dress rehearsal was definitely going smoothly—even if it would have been much better with the real Miriam onstage.

But that wasn't going to happen. At least not until the magic wind came to turn Katie back into herself.

× × ×

"Bye, Miriam. I bet you'll feel better tomorrow," Mandy Banks said as she left the girls' dressing room after the rehearsal.

Katie waved, but didn't say anything. After all, she was supposed to have laryngitis.

"Keep drinking that tea!" Ms. Sweet said as she placed the last costume on a hanger and walked toward the door. "We're really going to need you tomorrow."

"Don't forget you still have *me*," Suzanne said, zipping up her white winter parka.

"Oh, of course, Suzanne," Ms. Sweet assured her. "But we're all hoping Miriam will be well enough to go on tomorrow. She's worked so hard."

Suzanne frowned.

As Suzanne and Ms. Sweet left the dressing room, Katie sat there alone for a minute, staring at the mirror. Miriam's face stared back at her.

Just then Katie felt a cool breeze blowing on the back of her neck. She turned around to see if someone had come back into the dressing room.

But the door was shut tight.

The draft on Katie's neck grew colder then, and her hair started blowing.

But the costumes that were hanging up weren't moving with the wind at all. Neither were the scripts that were scattered around the room.

In fact, the wind only seemed to be blowing right on Katie. Which could only mean one thing . . .

The magic wind was back!

The wild tornado started blowing harder and harder now, whipping around and around, faster and faster until . . .

It stopped.

Just like that. The magic wind was gone and Katie Carew was back!

The real Miriam Chan was back, too. And boy, was she confused.

Chapter 12

"Katie?" Miriam asked slowly. She looked around. "How did I get here?"

"You . . . uh . . . you came in here after the rehearsal," Katie replied.

"*After* the rehearsal?" Miriam repeated. "You mean it's over?"

Katie nodded.

"But I . . . I don't remember . . ." Miriam began. Then she stopped. "Well, I sort of do. Kind of. I was up onstage, and then I was in the audience and . . . oh, I don't know. It's all sort of fuzzy."

"You got laryngitis," Katie told her. "But you sound better now."

"I guess," Miriam said.

"You're fine," Katie assured her. "And you're going to be amazing tomorrow."

"I sure hope so," Miriam told her. "I really wish that I had gotten a chance to do the dress rehearsal, because—"

Just then Suzanne burst into the dressing room. "Miriam! You're talking!" she exclaimed. She did not look happy about it.

"I thought you left," Katie said to Suzanne.

"I forgot my script." Suzanne turned toward Miriam. "How did you get your voice back so quickly?"

"Um . . . that tea was really powerful," Katie suggested.

Suzanne didn't seem very convinced. "You sure got your voice back pretty fast. The last time I had laryngitis I could hardly talk for three days!" Her eyes grew small and angry.

"I should get going," Miriam said. "I want to practice a few things tonight." She raced out of the room, away from Suzanne's angry glare.

"It's not fair!" Suzanne declared as Miriam left. "Why did she have to get her voice back?"

"That's not nice, Suzanne," Katie said.

"Yeah, well, it's not nice to tease a person and make her think she's going to have the lead in the play and then take it away," Suzanne shot back.

Katie thought about that. She could under-stand why Suzanne was upset.

And it *was* kind of Katie's fault. After all, she was the one who faked having laryngitis so she didn't have to go back onstage. If she hadn't done that, Suzanne wouldn't have got-ten her hopes up.

Suzanne really wanted to be a star. She loved attention. Unfortunately, Katie couldn't help her with that.

Or could she?

Suddenly Katie got another one of her great ideas.

"Suzanne, I think there's a way that you can be a star tomorrow night, too," she said.

"Yeah, right," Suzanne harrumphed.

"No, really. I have a plan," Katie told her. She grabbed Suzanne by the arm. "Come on. We need to talk to Mr. G. right now!"

Chapter 13

"One, two, a one, two, three, four!"

As soon as Mr. Starkey began to play the piano, the curtain went up, and Miriam danced across the stage singing her song. The audience applauded wildly.

"The scenery looks awesome!" Suzanne whispered to Katie and Mr. G.

Katie looked across the catwalk at Suzanne. "Thanks. Are you almost ready?"

Suzanne looked down at the stage. George and Kadeem were talking to each other. "I think so. I guess I'd better get ready to go on."

Katie nodded. "Break a leg," she said.

Suzanne nodded nervously as she got ready

to go onstage. "Thanks."

Just then the snowflake music began to play. Suzanne grabbed her sleigh bells and began to shake them. And then . . .

She pushed herself right off the catwalk!

But Suzanne didn't fall hard onto the wood floor below. Instead, she drifted slowly to the ground—just like a real snowflake!

And it was all thanks to Katie!

Strong ropes were attached to Suzanne's costume. Katie and Mr. G. worked together to gently lower her onto the stage—the same way Katie had learned to work the sun she'd made.

As Suzanne whirled and twirled in the air, the audience members jumped to their feet and cheered wildly.

Suzanne took a special bow as she landed. She smiled up at Katie.

Katie looked down and gave Suzanne a big thumbs-up. Suzanne wasn't the star of the play, but the audience was certainly going to remember her performance.

"Well, you certainly surprised me," Mr. Starkey told Suzanne backstage after the play had ended.

"Me too," Jeremy agreed. "I couldn't believe it when I saw you jump from that catwalk. I thought you were crazy."

"Were you scared?" Emma W. asked her.

Suzanne shook her head. "Not at all," she assured her, obviously enjoying all of the attention her surprise was getting.

"Where did you get the idea to do that?" Kevin wondered.

"I decided my entrance needed to be more spectacular. So I asked Katie and Mr. G. to help me with it," Suzanne explained.

Katie sighed. That wasn't exactly the way it had happened.

Just then Miriam walked backstage. She was carrying a big bouquet of roses. Surprisingly, Suzanne was the first to congratulate her.

"You were awesome, Miriam," Suzanne told her. "I'm so glad your voice came back."

"Th-thanks," Miriam stammered. She was shocked to get a compliment from Suzanne. "You were great, too."

"I know," Suzanne replied proudly.

"You really were amazing," Katie told Miriam. "Everyone is talking about what a great voice you have."

"Well, I never could have done it without you," Miriam told Katie. "After all, you were one of the people who convinced me to try out."

Katie gulped. She hadn't wanted Suzanne to know about that. But now that the secret was out, Katie braced herself for a big burst of Suzanne fury.

Surprisingly, Suzanne didn't seem mad. "I guess Katie helped both of us," she told Miriam sweetly.

"She sure did," Miriam agreed.

Suzanne turned to Katie. "So who do you

think got the most applause?" she asked her. "Miriam or me?"

Katie rolled her eyes. Suzanne never changed.

Still, it was sort of wonderful knowing that her best friend would always be the same.

With the magic wind around, that was something Katie couldn't say about herself. *Katie* changed all the time. One . . . two . . . switcheroo!

Chapter 14

Fingerprint Doodles

Katie's new favorite drawing projects are her fingerprint doodles. They are as unique as Katie is. After all, no two people have the same fingerprints. Which means no one will *ever* be able to make a fingerprint doodle that is exactly like yours!

Here's what you need:

Paper, an ink pad with washable ink, colored markers

Here's what you do:

1. Press your fingertip on an ink pad.

2. Roll your ink on a piece of paper to create a fingerprint.

3. Clean the ink off of your finger with soap and water.

4. Use a marker to create a picture from the fingerprint.

Here are two fun fingerprint doodle ideas from Katie:

• Add long brown dog ears, a dog nose, some brown and white curls, and a short, stubby tail to your fingerprint. Now you've got a Pepper picture!

• Draw black triangle-shaped ears, whiskers, and a long tail. *Meow*. Wow! That's Jeremy's black cat, Lucky.

About the Author

Nancy Krulik is the author of more than 150 books for children and young adults, including three *New York Times* best sellers. She lives in New York City with her husband, composer Daniel Burwasser, and their children, Amanda and Ian. When she's not busy writing the Katie Kazoo, Switcheroo series, Nancy loves swimming, reading, and going to the movies.

About the Illustrators

John & Wendy have illustrated all of the Katie Kazoo books, but when they're not busy drawing Katie and her friends, they like to paint, take photographs, travel, and play music in their rock 'n' roll band. They live and work in Brooklyn, New York.